Hello Children,

When I was small, about your age, I used to enjoy looking through picture books in search of all the small things that could be discovered within.

Today, although I am much older, I still remember how much I used to enjoy doing this. This is why I've thought up this special picture book. And to make it more exciting, I have hidden funny little things that don't exist or put things in the wrong place.

So, are you keen on searching for the mistakes?

Take note: Some things you will find easily, but others are really tricky and I have hidden them well. Of course, you can try finding all the mistakes on your own. But if you want to, you can have your friends, parents or grandparents join in. Then you can find out who really has good eyesight!

At the back of the book you will find all the illustrations again reduced in size. Here you can check to see if you have found all the mistakes. But don't cheat - try to find them on your own first.

OK?

I wish you all loads of fun.

Best wishes from

Ralf Butschkow

Ralf Butschkow

SOMETHING IS NOT QUITE RIGHT!

A find-the-mistake picture book

Kane/Miller
BOOK PUBLISHERS

Today is a day just like any other day. Lisa says "Good Morning" to her dog, Popcorn and her cat, Butter, as she gets dressed.

But just as Lisa is about to leave her room, she has a feeling that something is **different**.

Something is not quite right!

What could it be?
What is different?
Did she give her teddy bear his
good morning kiss?
Yes, just as she does
every morning.
So that's not it.

After breakfast Lisa and Popcorn go out to do some shopping. On the way, they walk past their favorite playground. But Lisa doesn't feel like playing today – she has some important thinking to do. She must figure out what it is that's not quite right.

"Did I remember to put on my underpants?" she asks herself. "No, that's not it. I would have noticed that! Maybe I put on two pairs by mistake?"

Lisa is thinking so hard that she doesn't notice the light change and misses her turn to cross the street!

Finally, Lisa and Popcorn reach the supermarket.
Lisa's mom has given her a list of what to buy:
vegetables, butter, and cornflakes. For
some reason it takes Lisa much longer
than usual to find everything.

On most days, Lisa stops at the building site to watch the workers, but today she doesn't feel like it. "Something is just not right," she thinks to herself. "I wish I could put my finger on what it is!"

PLEASE WIPE
YOUR FEET!

"Is it Mom's birthday today? Did I forget to buy her a present? No, it can't be that," Lisa thinks. "Mom's birthday is in winter, when it's cold outside."

By the harbor, Lisa doesn't even stop to throw pebbles
into the water like she normally does.
"Maybe I forgot to feed my fish this morning?"
she mumbles. But no, as usual, Lisa fed them.

In the evening when she's brushing her teeth, Lisa still wonders what it is that has been different all day. Maybe she just got up on the wrong side of the bed.

Time for bed. Lisa takes off her shoes, wiggles her feet, and...that's it! She has been wearing two different socks all day long!

"Well, well," Lisa sighs happily.
"I knew something was not quite right!"

Did you find all the mistakes?
Here are the answers.

Eating breakfast

The playground

On the street

In the supermarket

The building site

Walking home

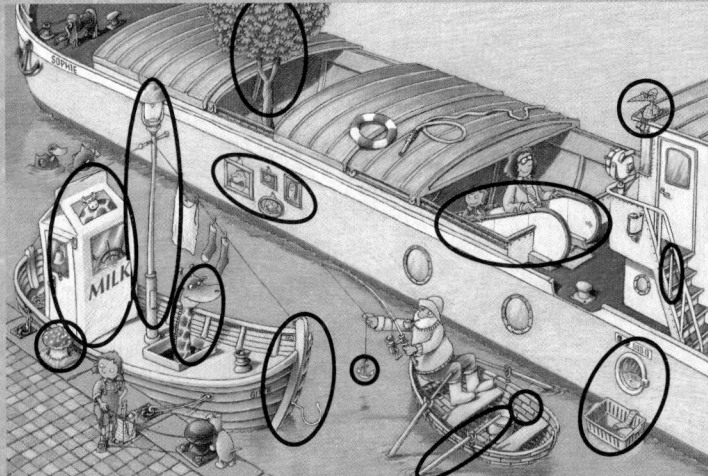

The harbor

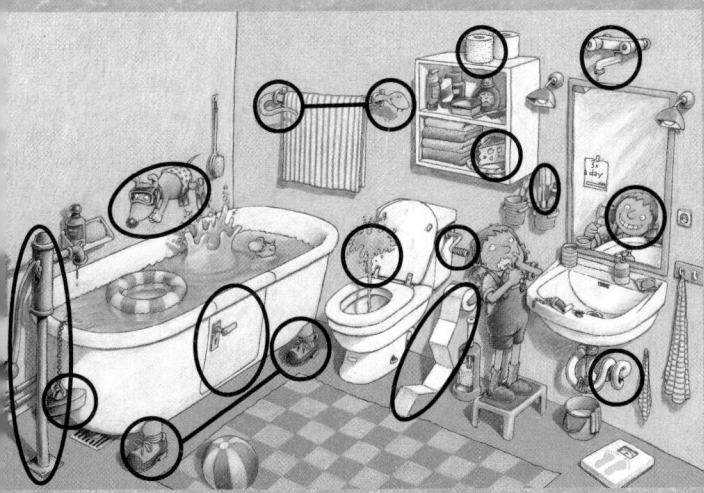

The bathroom

Lisa's bedroom

First American Edition 2002
by Kane/Miller Book Publishers
La Jolla, California

Originally published in Germany in 2001 under the title *Da Stimmt doch Was Nicht!*
By Baumhaus Medien AG, Frankfurt

Library of Congress Control Number: 2001099520
ISBN: 1-929132-29-8
Printed and bound in Germany by J. P. Himmer GmbH, Augsburg
1 2 3 4 5 6 7 8 9 10